Neighborhoods

A Collage

by Penn Schaw

Neighborhoods
A Collage

Chapter 1

Whenever you wish for a happy story, NEVER spoil the story with the truth!

How many times in a leisurely moment do we nostalgically recall life as a simpler more carefree time filled with neighborhood friends playing kick-the-can, hopscotch, or baseball in the street? Can this fantasy of small town sweetness, translate into somewhat the same attitudes throughout our neighborhoods?

Upon closer examination the small town neighborhoods of our past may still exist within cities, but if fractured, what type of disruptive thinking will help rebuild our neighborhoods?

In tiny towns, little villages, large cities, where do our great neighborhoods fit? Spanish Harlem is a small neighborhood in a metropolitan city: New York City. Then there are the ghost towns, large or small, which have one thing in common, no people. People can be and are disruptive as in most any group.

Build on an earthquakes' fault line, in a tsunami-flood zone, in an avalanche zone and you can almost guarantee that you'll be trying to put

Humpty Dumpty back together again. But remember that people, along with Mother Nature, are very disruptive forces. You're civil at times, not so civil at other times, but it's peoples' attitudes and actions which can create pleasure or strife. Yet when serious calamities strike, these neighborhoods do briefly draw together and are supportive, out of need.

Chapter 2

Whether Spanish Harlem or Goldbeach, Oregon, your neighborhood, your village, your future nostalgic memory is where you live.

Are these villages and neighborhoods the forgotten "villas" of this country, this world and our civilizations? How silly it is of us to almost ignore having pride in where we live. Most of the time we seem to care more about strip centers, boardwalks and the glittering high life of downtowns. It's almost as if we have to run away from ourselves, whether traveling, watching TV, or getting jobs in the big city, etc. to entertain ourselves. Where are the pre-radio homes, hearths, music, piano and creative spirit of yesteryear? It still exists, but you have to find it. Virtual offices, virtual rock concerts, virtual searches and other tribal events are bringing back some of that spirited feeling.

A high desert cowboy and his attractive wife were eating dinner in a small town café. He was describing his feeling of joy just being and living in the remote high desert of far northern Nevada. What serenity there is living in the vast expanse of a sparsely populated desert. When asked, he described his view of city life, "A city reminds me of a huge ant hill in a remote desert. You kick the ant hill and all of a sudden you see a vast number of swarming ants!" (his description of a city.)

It is said that if you slice and dice areas of influence into sixteen square blocks, with known boundaries you could have meaningful, functional communities or neighborhoods. Plato might say, "A group of less than 6,000 people could be manageable as a neighborhood." A certain familiarity, ethnic or otherwise can possibly, with work, breed respect, but you have to work on pride and respect a whole lot.

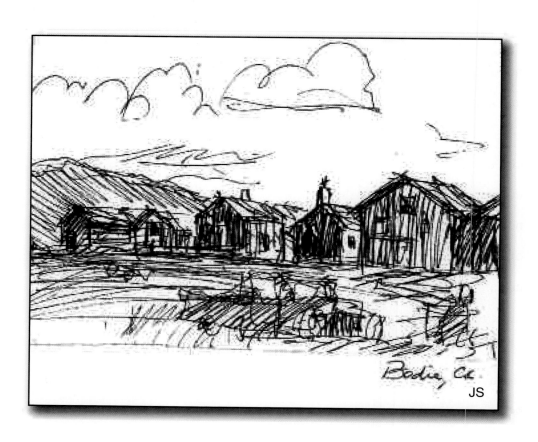

Bodie, CA.
JS

Chapter 3

Clang, clang, hot dang! Where am I, on a train, on a trolley or just out on Fulton's Folly? Can it be said that there are few if any answers, for ways to achieve, the bliss of living in a village, town, or small metropolitan neighborhood? Upon closer examination they too have warts, knife fights, burglaries, and martial disputes. Oh what the hell, nothing is perfect!

What about ghost towns? No people, no fights, nothing doing? Not so. Granted, how can you have crime without people? But if there is nothing doing in ghost towns then there should only be the pure boredom of nothingness. Witness the swarms of people, not ants, who go to the ghost town of Bodie, Calif. and think otherwise. They go in part in their quest of the nostalgia and simplicity of yesteryear. This yearning helps to create the excitement of doing for these folks.

Each, when asked, "What do you know about boredom?" the professional or the five year old might reply, "I just don't have time to think about boredom, I just Do."

The Hoovers of Stanford University with their palatial shack next to the Standard (gold) Mine in Bodie enjoyed a westward view of the alpine high mountains in the Hoover Wilderness area next to Yosemite Park. Few knew of this view from Bodie, but the Hoover's did. How important is the view you have in your own neighborhood? The trees, the gardens, the home designs, the skylines, and of course the variety of people. The Hoover's also knew about Tesla coils (AC electricity). In Bodie there is a light bulb that has been continuously burning since before 1930. A light bulb that has never been turned off!

How can your attitude be positively lit to bring your ghostly neighborhood into the light of day? Community needs communication, recognition and respect for the folks residing there, as well as sources for retreat and rest.

Hop on that train, let the light shine on your depth of knowledge, expand your thoughts and broaden your view of the future.

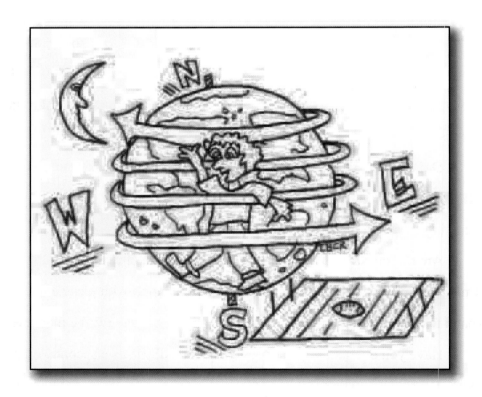

Chapter 4

Think of Billy at the age of six arriving in the farmland of his mother's friend's farm near Walla Walla, Washington. A city boy from Seattle suddenly transported to another world, a world with room to smell the wheat, and misbehave. We all do, you know!

What did he think when he first saw the huge motorized harvesters and threshers? Did they first appear as Jules Verne type vehicles floating across the fields? The magic of these magnificent, man-driven machines moving without the aid of horses could have been a pivotal moment in Billy's life. A young man standing in a vast field suddenly realizing that anything is possible.

Did these and other seemingly insignificant events combine to spark a fire within his being? Did he realize at the time that this simple insight might light his future and the future of the world?

Did he recall those moments when he decided, years later, to drop out of Harvard in creative pursuit of magic machines and codes not only capable of floating across fields, but around the world?

Are our quests to create sparks of insight fanned by a pride of farmland, village, and neighborhood. Our identification with place can expand to include mountains, continents and even our place in the universe.

Have you ever been asked how many football fields a second you are moving, at this latitude and in which direction east or west, as the earth rotates?

Do not take into account the other motions of the earth and sun through the universe in your answer.

Some might ask, "Do you really know where you are?"

Good luck.

Chapter 5

Jack spent his sub-teen years in a small coastal town. The world beyond his backyard chain link fence consisted of a huge field, a rail line and a railroad repair yard.

It was not the most sophisticated or desirable address to be included in the local social register of the town. But for Jack, his backdoor opened not on a less desirable location, but onto a world filled with mystery and fascination. Where had these railcars come from? What had they seen? Where were they going? Would someday Jack be privy to their adventures and secret lives beyond his backyard?

Jack's town had a couple of other claims to fame. There was a house filled with ghosts and in the bay was an actual Japanese submarine. Otherwise it was just a typical village with a school, library, post office, small hotel, coffee shop, restaurant, bakery, club house, a few churches, and a museum. For Jack it was the perfect place, where his young mind could conjure up vast fantasies, which then could be played out with friends in daily play and eventually in his future.

As a young Germanic type in the early 1940s he sensed the prejudice that was rampant almost everywhere. Fortunately his family had home entertainment, fine grammar and excellent high school teachers, his parents. Perhaps as a result of the times Jack and his sister Jill, were frequently jolted into moving to slightly larger villages and then to an actual town.

Along the way to adulthood Slap Jack became acquainted with larger farming villages and towns. At one time Jack lived in a river town, somewhat like Huck Finn's Hannibal, Missouri. The town had one very unique feature, it was situated at the end of the trans Pacific jet stream. Looking skyward you could sometimes see balloons dropping from their indiscriminate flight paths across the ocean. These balloons were carrying bombs which usually landed and exploded in the fields and orchards near town. They carried feelings of terror and the threat of potential attack for the adults. For a young man they also were heavily laden with excitement and adventure.

Everyone knew the balloons were relatively safe, if you stayed clear when they landed. No deaths occurred until after World War II. A dud bomb exploded and one adult and five children were killed, while examining the fallen balloon, when on a picnic near Bly, Oregon. The event served as a warning that even in the pristine and peaceful country-side danger could be lurking.

The memory of this experience served the community of Bly very well when in 2002, a Mideast terrorist training camp was discovered being built outside of town. The community of Bly stopped the camps' formation in its tracks.

Jack, the little boy grew up, if not on the wrong side of the tracks, at least near the tracks. Railroads and balloons raining possible death, small town adventures and excitement set the stage for his future.

Jack became a world famous architect. Recalling the fascination of his railroad roots, he helped design the new underground and above ground railway stations for the city of Hong Kong.

Chapter 6

Training wheels on steroids can explode etiquette?! Finger foods in people's paws can surpass infancy. So why are the knives, forks, spoons, and chopsticks so essential to the restaurant crowd and why can't an individual's neighborhood project its own style? As an example, why not include within the neighborhood a few tent camps, homeless enclaves, and protesters? Wouldn't these groups and events be a bit like having the excitement of a rodeo and less like the conditioning of a Rodeo Drive?

A rack or racks of lambs (people) could be quite gruesome in Medieval times, just as in certain spots around the world today. Civilizations and neighborhoods may need limits because they desire some limits. Could Henry the VIII and Mozart help describe a few limits or boundaries? Think of Mozart as a great composer with warts and Henry the VIII as a serial killer. Guess who would you like to have living within your sixteen square block neighborhood? Which chap would HURT OR NOT HURT, HELP OR NOT HELP in your community? The choice of ethics is yours!

Buy some chaps, borrow a horse, put on your cowboy boots, bring out a lasso and try to rope a calf. Roping in an urban neighborhood might seem out of place, but is eating food with your fingers any less unusual?

The infant has few eating boundaries and the lack of these boundaries hurts few if any citizens, unless you're perhaps politically correct, whatever that means.

So the drum song of humanity goes on and on in a neighborhood that is small enough, even within a large city. This song can be as manageable and melodious as an un-kicked ant hill in the high desert; if the attitude of you and your neighbors provide for community, diversity, and harmony.

Chapter 7

The security guard in front of our small town bank wasn't threatened by any Wall Street groups. Quick Draw has a very high IQ and a warm loving heart. He wouldn't hurt a flea, but no one knew that. He was trained to write down license plate numbers on cars in the bank parking lot and to greet customers with the expression, "Have a nice day." If you asked him to tell you to "Have a bad day," he just couldn't and wouldn't say it.

Like Ken and Barbie dolls, you pull the cord attached to their backs and the thoughtless spiel pours out, "Have a nice day. Have a nice day." The expression may not be shallow, but the robotic-like responses sometimes are.

Do you feel as if there is little depth or true meaning to this inane expression other than wanting to project a cheery feeling to sometimes lonely people. Roy Orbison of Wink, Texas, population 200, came up with the lyrics and song, "Only the Lonely People." Just think you, your friends and even Quick Draw could be the lonely people.

At first Quick Draw didn't know how to use his piece. Practice at the local rifle range changed things rapidly for him. Valiant motives urged him on. Squirrel hunting by sharp shooters to save hay and alfalfa farmers from bankruptcy was an example. He wanted to help the farmers stay in business. Even with his high level and newly developed skills, like the buffalo, the squirrels began to disappear. But Quick Draw could not save any bank from bankruptcy. Only too late did he discover that the desperados could be inside the bank, all along.

A lady in a tony, vegan grocery store, complete with butcher shop, heard Quick Draw, now an elk hunter, boast about his kill of a 650 lb. when fully dressed elk with a huge rack. The lady had just purchased three T-bone steaks with great marbling. She cringed and condescendingly exclaimed to Quick Draw, "You shot a helpless elk!"

He turned to her and asked, "Didn't you just buy some steaks?"

Her response was, "But mine are manufactured."

Are we conditioned by our experiences and culture?

Chapter 8

What is limited wisdom?

No one I know in the flesh has more than limited wisdom. The question is not what is the limit to wisdom? People may have a lot of facts, some knowledge, and all the headaches of the day.

A painless Potter does not exist, but many tinker, tailor magic players (that's you) are hopeful doers. The mistake ridden player, who walks that fine line, who time after time slams against a closed door, will have scars. But the player will also have the greater knowledge of what mistakes, luck and even persistence can bring to the table.

If you don't try, how can you know? How can you live, other than to just hide from people?

Contemplation, silence and serenity are just fine, so never disrespect day dreaming and where your dreams may lead.

If you do apps, make sure they're earth shaking.

Rick, the programmer designed, coded, and presented the earth shaking, spinning global app showing where and the intensity of earthquakes, as they occur. Each click and the lubricant of resulting money helps Rick achieve a greater freedom to do something new and exciting. Rick has no Midas pile of gold, there's too much to do.

I'm a ten year old or a sixty year old tinkerer who needs 3D toys to manhandle and perhaps destroy, but I have to hold and manipulate the parts first.

Penny, a teacher with a hard science Ph.D., has figured this out; Book Toys, sciencewiz.com. Tactile touch can lead to "hands on" joy with tools for making and baking ideas!

Sadness prevails when some big investment banker, some venture capitalist, or some hedge fund types help crush a company which can be competition to their pet projects. The desire for power and or control is vicious. Beware of the provider of cheap money who wants to control you, or perhaps capture your valuable patents pending or other work product.

There are early search engines that were crushed out of existence. The intense greed of some does hurt inventive types. The legion of do gooders are few and far between. The not so neighborly types abound!

Chapter 9

The nest is the neighborhood and the home.

Try homeward bound. Your block watch can be a collaboration of familiarity, breeding safety. You easily recognize the folks on your block and can therefore spot the intruder, the stranger, the possible thief nearby. Watch birds with young ones, protecting their nests by trying to drive away predators. Mother Nature is encoded into a fabric of existence and survival.

Let's look into Bloomberg, the news service, or Blomberg, the Swedish construction foreman, or should we just get to the real nitty-gritty. Look to the cycles of the moon, the effects of the sun, the energy of the star systems, the Milky Way, our cosmos, which all seem to be birthing and creating systems. Refer to the planet and some astrological signs or even to Sir Isaac Newton's favorite, alchemy. Read your horoscope to help fill this universal joy and mystery. Call it creating, birthing and love, that's how you got here!

At least half the human population has very, very intimate and advanced creating and birthing skills. The allure of the continuation of the human race and the creation of you, certainly has a lot to do with what we call women. Women's work is never done and hopefully the work is done in a protected environment, a comfortable, small neighborhood and home.

Let's vote for the small comfortable neighborhood in cities too!

Chapter 10

You've probably played post office in school. There is now a new game called Shrink the Post Office. Let's get rid of the 3,000 plus post offices in neighborhoods, villages, towns and lowly attended big city post offices. Forget the fact that many of these post offices don't have home delivery, and that closing them would expand the distance through winter's snow and ice just to get your mail. Oh happy days! For the price of a B-1 bomber or Two, these post offices might stay, and gas consumption of both plane and car could at least stay stable. Rip the post office out of rural towns, villages, or elsewhere, and you have created havoc in the neighborhood!

Post offices create employment and are the most immediate face of the Federal government. You may know these folks and you'd hate to see them move or be unemployed. Today's pictures of Bermuda, Hawaii, and other decorations, which may show the jolly humanness of these postal folk, are being removed from their cubicles at post offices on the premise that post offices must conform and look somewhat the same. What idiotic bureaucrats make rules that turn human beings almost into robots? Is that what you want them to be?

Watch the letter sorter who doesn't have a sorting machine become really nervous. Computer time schedules must be met; some irrelevant reports never required before or read again, must be filled in and computerized. When do the postal folks have time to talk with you the customers, the ones who really count? They don't. Bye, bye, a public relations fiasco!

Some seem to think that the post offices aren't one of the central hubs for the village and or the neighborhood. Ever stop to think why it might take hours just to get your mail in a small town? It's not the hordes of customers waiting in line to buy a stamp.

Why can't some genius figure out that the customers talk to other customers? Jobs may be lost as true networking locations are diminished. Urgent help, assistance and knowledge can come from post offices, fire stations, and other central points of community in almost every neighborhood or village.

Keep them!

Chapter 11

Whether in a ghost town, a Neanderthal village, or metropolitan city, why can't we have a small tent camp in our neighborhood?

Our neighborhood park has dog walks and off leash areas with plastic bags for collection. Why can't we treat our protesters and other human beings at least to a dog's life and maybe even upgrade them to tent camps?

In the 1880s the very socially sophisticated San Francisco tourist would travel to Beebright by the Sea, paying money to tent camp in luxury for the holidays. Have we forgotten how to treat people with and without hotels and motels? Yosemite Park, to this day, has the Curry tent camp with only outdoor plumbing. There are no toilets or sinks in the tents. If the U.S. Army, the Federal government and others can run tent camps with only electricity, Coleman lanterns or candles, why can't we?

Is the fear of being too primitive so ingrained in our planning departments that the idea of respectable housing including tent camps are literally thrown out the window with inane codes and regulations? Don't allow them to. Do we really believe that Yurts don't work? Ask the Turkic nomads. Why is there a waiting list at times for the tents at the Curry tent camp in Yosemite? Is the fire town of "Burning Man," which grows from zero population to more than fifty thousand people in a little over a month and then disappears, devoid of tents? Go to Gerlach, Nevada and ask about crime, wildfires and tents at

Burning Man. What you get is a loving smile. There is little if any crime and many inventive spirits inhabiting the Black Rock Desert's Burning Man. Ask a few architects, the founders of Google, and many, many high tech leaders about living in dust storms in the harsh high desert. Don't ignore a woman's response to Burning Man by Lady Bee.

Tents are not just for boy and girl scouts who go off to the high mountain retreats and other recreational areas. Why spend so much time and money on travel when you can tent camp in the city, or just sleep under the stars as people have done for thousands of years?

Bring the country back to the city and not just in secret backyard camping. Imagine Sierra Club members, many who are city and town residents, giving some of their energy back to the neighborhood to recreate the wilderness experience of tent camps. Of course if they don't want to do this, there are legions of Native Americans who can. The knowledge is there.

How politically correct and incompetent can we be to avoid the excitement of tent camp and tepees in the neighborhood, along with neighborhood forums and town hall meetings? Population is small in neighborhoods and can be heard, yes, where we live. We therefore can raise our voices, our consciousness and our pride where we live, in our neighborhood.

Chapter 12

Downtown in the streets of Laredo there's a Texas Tea House or two. Café society begins at 6 A.M. The professor knows that this is better than a roundup room. Theodore, a Texas treat known as the evictor, begs his bouncer, the handsome Joaquin, to take out the oatmeal muncher. Ashley bats her eyes, and as Joaquin is distracted, the double, double, triple, triple, on secret probation oatmeal muncher suddenly suspends Theodore, the café owner, from the rafters by his suspenders. Carla pleads for her husband's sake and safety. This fairly standard morning episode at our breakfast café can create a noisy day. Even the N.Y. Times newspaper sends a reporter by.

Begin the day with Benny, a 6 A.M. regular not being at the café that morning. Something must be terribly wrong and desperate at the harbor if Benny's not here. In the quiet of early morning the Harbor Master gets real busy around 4 A.M. towing sailboats out to sea. At 7 A.M. you have a very, very low tide and flopping fish. By 9 A.M. helicopters are overhead thump, thumping. Their television cameras show looky-looks on the bridge over the harbor eyeing a yacht floating upside down in the half-mile long harbor playing bumper tag in troubled waters. While there is at least ten million dollars of damage to piers, sailboats, fishing boats and yachts, that ain't much. Fukushima, with an earthquake, then a tsunami had just sent waves across the Pacific Ocean to our own little neighborhood. What next?

Ben missed morning coffee, but saved the insurance companies millions of dollars. After years of hard work he was retired, a job well done.

A year or so before, low flying helicopters sprayed chemicals over our neighborhood to OFF the Australian Gray Moth. To Robert, a tough European emigrant, the thumping sounds of a helicopter flying over our homes reminded him of a bombing run over Copenhagen, Denmark during WWII. When Robert was a little boy, the bombing runs created horrible memories and continued nightmares. Now the new "mare" occurs after a few helicopters armed with a not so inert gas spray for moths and us. Shades of the past, remember the Mediterranean fruit fly spraying and bombing.

Eventually Robert left his nightmares behind, but will our neighborhood or café ever be quite the same?

Suspense or suspenders, this morning café-community clearing house is an important part of the fabric of our neighborhood

How about yours?

Chapter 13

You usually can pick out an invader or tourist in the café or in the crowd. At early morning sunrise the invasion of a low slung bicycle, not tank, on our streets had this driver all shook up. As I slammed on the brakes of my hybrid Royota, this low slung, two wheeled infernal machine, with its, "on a pole rising sun" waving flag flashed by. The flag saved the bicyclist, bug doctor from a wreck or worse. Weaving in and out of cars at the cliff's edge, like a giant dragonfly, he had been watching spouting whales in the ocean and had not been paying attention to the busy street.

The police accident report was lengthy concerning our intruder. It was found he was a wrestler on a bike, but no Gorgeous George type. In fact, back in time, the wonderful town of Dinuba could only put up with the guy for at most a year or two. Dinuba, a small valley town, has the distinction of having farms nearby, Mexican velvet paintings selling at crossroads, no bars, and the tinkerer Rutan, in his youth, building stick model airplanes and rockets. Later Lord Branson finds the dude Rutan, who will become the winner of the Saint Louis X prize. If the wrestler doesn't know, that's not an Oklahoma windmill or a Missouri mule.

The inner-outer space prize went to a small town kid who unlike Tom Edison in his youth had no reason to fear railroad trains with conductors who could box your ears. The hurting bully left Tom almost completely deaf, but certainly not dumb. After all, we've still got his music records and much, much more.

The X prize, if it doesn't already, should include a sculpture of a rocket on its way to space. But the great dragonfly, bicycle riding, bug doctor surely deserves a sculpture of himself in a garden at a museum, complete with a frog or two, glaring and croaking for good measure. End of report.

Chapter 14

There are Victory gardens, vegetable gardens, organic gardens, arboretums, parks and perhaps even virtual gardens.

But "Jack and the Bean Stalk" bloomers, who can they be?

Maybe some attend grammar school in our neighborhood. This is a time when young ones can really grow and for some, grow really Bored. The town mayor, not in our neighborhood, but in the town, took on some tough twelve to fifteen year old youngsters. Instead of using the "off to reform school" approach, he set them up with computers, great teachers, and contracts to perform. You weren't allowed to call da mayor to complain that you had too much homework, or the class was too noisy or that the teacher was too mean. But you could phone him if you were truly bored. That probably meant that the teacher wasn't a good salesperson, he or she wasn't selling the course content in a meaningful and exciting way. In da mayor's school more than 80% of these tough guys and gals went on to community colleges or beyond.

Should first graders be taught a course in how to deal with boredom, after all we teach young children how to read and the grueling job of how to write? In my first grade class we had twenty-two right-handers and one lefty, me. My mind is crippled now and I'm perhaps dyslexic. The entire class was, by golly, right handed by the year's end. Hooray, welcome to the administrative bureaucracy. The rules are the rules after all. Right brain and left brain thinking may be a skill set we all aspire to. Can we change that too? Let's stop teaching art, music and sports?

You are close up and personal in your neighborhood, the school or schools in your neighborhood are not far away. Go find the teachers, the schools, the students and enrich yourself.

Chapter 15

If you had a wish list for your neighborhood, what would be on your list? What would you do?

After jobs, lack of strife and a nurturing hearth, the view could be an essential item. Visual thinking, "A Picture is Worth a Thousand Words," could be a place to look. People keep escaping to the mountains, the lakes, the ocean and the desert for many reasons. Perhaps the terrain is too harsh, particularly on the brain's eyes.

A lad from Los Angeles, who had it all, moved to Seattle because the distance from L.A. to the closest recreational areas was just too far away.

In Seattle, Mother Nature's eye candy, the Cascades, Mt. Rainier, Shaw and the San Juan Islands, the Olympic Peninsula, were all close by and easily accessible.

What can you do when your area isn't richly endowed?

Take this visual thinking one step further and bring the eye candy into the villages and towns. Without becoming a theme park, require the landscape architects to plant trees, shrubs, vegetable gardens and flower beds. Insist that all the designers study the art history of the area. Free these architects to use their visual thinking skills, free them from all but the most critical and essential building codes. Require that no more cookie cutter, same old, same old design monotonous, monstrosities be built. Even though seemingly more expensive at the time, the diversities in designs, not hectic, could help quiet the mind and reduce the crime! Reducing crime can lower economic costs in the long run. Stone masons, artists, carpenters, plumbers and many other craft-persons could see their work product begin to affect the communities, particularly the neighborhoods in which they live.

The internal centers of severely unhealthy cities might even be bulldozed to create organic farms with trailer parks, tent camps, and small self-contained villages (Beaux-Arts) on the periphery. An unimaginative city planner could even be fired in order to let loose a more imaginative visual thinker or thinkers. Robert Moses did a lot of redesign in New York City. Moritz Hauptmann helped recreate Paris at an earlier time, John McClaren with Fredrick Law Olmstead's additive skills landscaped and designed Golden Gate Park in San Francisco, and on and on. To the naysayer, who says rebuilding or building just can't be done quickly, look to Henry Kaiser and the Godfather movie set. Fleur Du Lac at Lake Tahoe was built in very short order on very marshy land. Look into the Burning Man's Black Rock City, which is erected in less than one month and then torn down in less than a month, every year.

Hello Naysayers! "Stuff can be done, as it is being done, at Burning Man by architects, innovative artists, fire dancers, and many, many more," said Lady Bee.

Who? Go search on "Google."

Chapter 16

The intergalactic hybrids arrived in your village to act. The inter-galactics didn't need to spray the town with laughing gas. We already have UFOs, sightseers, and dog and people walkers. No doubt our neighborhood needs to be taken off its leash. Dog and people walkers okay, but squirrel patrols, no.

Henry, our pet skunk, had his ways to chew through wire mesh vents at our home. Henry now has a permanent home as our marriage counselor, under our house. The inter-galactics know that if there's too much marital strife, Henry lets go and his wonderful scent filters up through the furnace vents. Should I say we are a home of quiet marital bliss!

Down the street from Leon, our taco truck driver, there prowled a fear-some mountain lion (puma). There are missing cats and dogs and even raccoons and rats. The fearsome puma even off-ed (killed) a kid or two of our neighbor's goats. What next?

Oh, our so orderly, so called civilized city can't even protect its neighborhoods from this menace, but it can require we humanoids follow endless numbers of over civilizing rules.

Thank God Leon hauled in a bear trapper from Montana to corral our wildlife. Leon, by taking charge, might very well have saved a kid's life, possibly yours! Thank you Leon and thanks to our bear trapper, whose ancient skill is coming back.

We need jobs now, but not reckless rules on how to behave or excessive fines to pad some bureaucrat's paycheck or to fund extended travels to

Washington D.C. and beyond. Can the gas pump laws of Oregon, where the attendant must pump your gas, not you, be expanded to most every state in the United States? Is it possible 250,000, 500,000 or a 1,000,000 entry level jobs could be created overnight?

Think about all the car wash jobs, hand drying cars, which have been created. Let George do it, now, in Washington. My wife is terrified to pump her own gas at a filling station; she has to, "rely on the kindness of strangers." Then there's the cigarette smoking, gas pumping, stupid, very explosive guy. I hope you're not there! Get going George! Don't spray the laughing gas over the legislature, please? Really almost like waving a wand, the legislature could create a national gas pumping law. The legislature then could have the last laugh by helping create up to a 1,000,000 Entry Level Jobs.

Chapter 17

Teaching in our small home town in the 1930s was like being in a cultural time warp. In our village of One Pine, where the thought of politically correct seemed not to exist, yet we existed.

Norman, our teacher in the seventh grade was a steep alpine mountain climber and a search and rescue expert. He never discussed his prowess. He didn't need to. If you have climbed at least ten, 12,000 foot no named peaks for the first ever time, with the exception of the Indians, you have a very rare skill set. To be able to locate a frozen cadaver of a lost hiker at 13,000 feet, when others for many months had failed, was beyond just ok.

Norman had another skill that he displayed in his eighth grade class-room. In the three room school house in our rugged western town, there could be shouting and more. A ruckus, a shout down, an explosion or worse could happen at any time, but never in Norman's quiet class. If a student threw chalk at the blackboard or at Norman's back, or set off a firecracker or a tiny black powder bomb for the flash effect, Norman could handle this commotion. There was no rush for security, rule books or swat squads for Norm. They didn't exist, but Norman had a pretty calm classroom, with a lot of holes in the ceiling. Why? The real silencer was Norman's 38 caliber six shooter, always at the ready. Start a ruckus in class and with one shot straight up into the ceiling, the classroom became suddenly silent. Surprisingly, the parents never complained.

It seems that pampering students is the politically correct way to control in the classrooms today. What Psychological damage, lawsuits and maybe even severe physical damage occurs today in the classroom due to enhanced pampering and little, if any, gunfire?

In another school, in 1990 to today, potential delinquents and delinquents actually excel. In this "down by the Delta" school, there are computers instead of guns, skilled teachers who love their work, caring but not intrusive parents, and students who sign contracts that help guide their responsibilities for the privilege of attending school. A new type of pride is beginning to emerge.

It's all in the doing.

Chapter 18

All that glistens is not gold, even in small villages and dairy farms.

Methane Mary, quite contrary, lets her cow pad ferment. For years her dairy farm near Tamale Bay has made milk into cheese and cow pads into pain. Methane pollution at her dairy fouls the sky through what was once pristine farmland. For the sake of health, let's sequester this carbon, produce energy and carbonize fiberboard. Cutting these methane and carbon plumes in modern days, will help keep our nearby village untainted, while still enjoying fresh cheese.

Methane in the atmosphere, that monster, was unknown to science many years ago. But cancer was obvious even way back then. Boost cattle production and their by-product methane, then concerns might grow about cancer. Sequester methane!

After Hiroshima many of the victims who survived digested miso to leech heavy metals from their bodies. Perhaps it was a fad or an old wives tale, but many radiation victims survived on miso soup with veggies.

Let's now discuss a ghost town in training, a dying village by Tamale Bay. Goodbye fishing fleets, oyster beds, and jobs, jobs, jobs. Healthy air and healthy villages go hand in hand. Copy Canada's fish farms by renewing oyster beds, and sequestering dairy methane gas into wallboard. Create those jobs, jobs, jobs. Jobs translate into happier and healthier times and towns. Folk who like the Tamale Village won't be forced to flee to the big cities to find work, but can rebuild their village, reintroduce or keep their small post office, and have fun doing so. Why not? We are crazy not to rebuild!

Way back when, the clear sky and beautiful skyline in the countryside hid the carbon, the methane and other small particulates. The idea of out of sight, out of mind worked. Today we can go far beyond Reasonable Containment and drive many jobs overseas or to unknown oblivion.

The soon to be released book, "Employ America," by Gordon Zuckerman could be a real catchword, a real goal of labor unions, corporations and the common folk.

It's time for a string theory, good vibrations, and a fifth dimension. Old invisible ghost towns could become viable and visible, as towns and jobs begin to reappear.

Chapter 19

Some illustrious folk on TV said that we can judge people by their zip code. How robotic can this be? Increasing the indifference levels of society are particularly symptomatic of large groups, cities, and huge universities. These self-proclaimed automaton-like groups really become almost robots themselves steered by the illustrious. Are these illustrious folk among those who could care less about you by thinking only of you as a zip code number?

Back in Dodge City, my neighborhood, this six-year olds' turf, life centered around the grammar school and its playground. The drugstore soda fountain, the neighborhood grocery store, the barber shop, the ghostly cemetery, the fire station, the park, the railroad tracks and repair yard all helped define our neighborhood's periphery. And without a high school, we still survived in our neighborhood. We had our secret hideouts, baseball diamonds, sidewalks, bike paths and a 60-yard football field that we painted with yard markers and stripes on our city street. The football field was almost perfect.

Of course the illustrious tried unsuccessfully to remove the stripes and yard markers, and therefore football was fun on our block for many years. Hooray!

Robert's Rules of Order are supposed to keep the barbarians with varied viewpoints from clashing. These rules can dumb down substantial opposing thoughts. Robert's rules may be a type of Pabulum pill that can hypnotize and quiet a crowd, but the embers of thought seem always to smolder in the background.

When you need to teach about crowd control and boundaries to civilization, smaller groups have a better chance to interact in these arenas.

We six-year olds knew when our bully tried to overpower us and our turf and boundaries.. The greatest hurt we could inflict on this bully was just to ignore the S.O.B. Surprise, in doing so, we helped our bully and his ego and evil quickly disappeared. This uncivil bully is now a popular civil friend! And remember we didn't have to have indifferent zip codes to define us and where we lived! Do you?

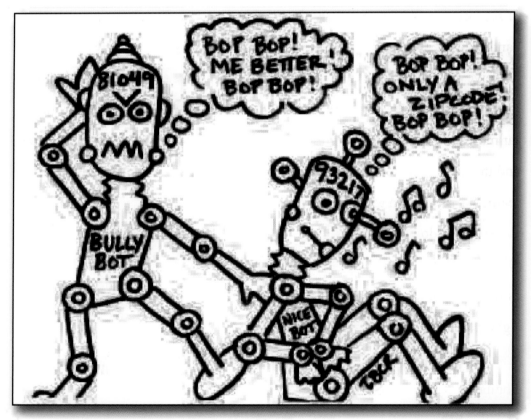

Chapter 20

Trip the LIGHT fantastic, dance a jig, take a swig, soul the train, and Please, Please Dream. What's wrong with a Billy Bong or even Hong Kong? Now, now, we must be correct and march on through life with love in our hearts! But do we? Hell no! If we started first loving our neighborhood, could we then infect larger communities and countries with our attitudes of collaboration and love? Maybe, maybe not, but we can try. Dream on!

Face the book, text the next, or ogle with "Google," and a new universe of activity opens up. One could say that "we have the whole world in our hands," but we forgot to wash them. I'll be a dirty dog, and the world can be perceived as rather dirty too. Suddenly dirt became far more apparent in this digital electronic age. IED's, car bombers and other folk became unfortunately far more real, but ostracized in our virtual world. What next? Dreaming of this and that at times can become a reality. Icarus, Orvil and Wilbur Wright all learned to fly, one in text and the others in the sky.

How do we play in the fifth dimension, which includes imagination? Didn't Superman say "faster than a speeding bullet," faster than light? If you've got something "faster than a speeding bullet" or even the speed of light, perhaps it's your imagination.

Sleep on this thought, dream on it, then, wake up. Educate the bombers.

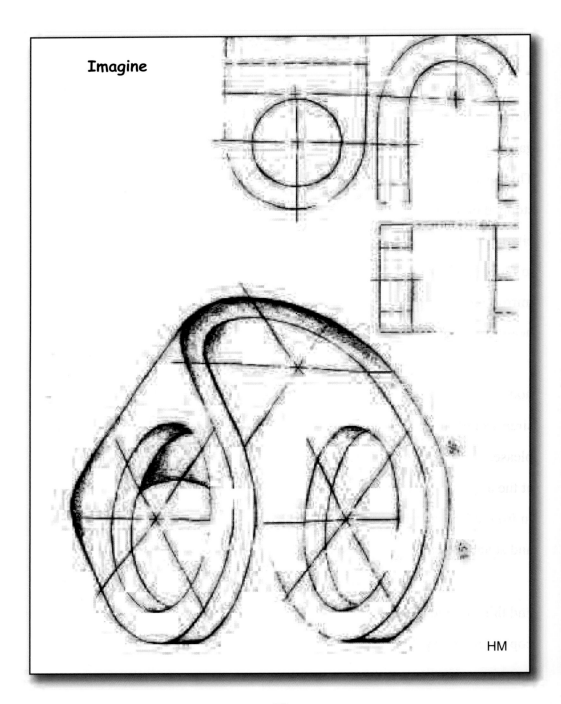

Imagine

HM

Chapter 21

The Wall Streeter populated village in the Hamptons on Long Island, New York, was a sitting duck. With its showcase monster houses and some gated communities it was a slam dunk place to set up an Obesity Check Point. This was not a DUI testing stop. No, this was the real deal. If you were stopped on Fatty Lane with your roly-poly ten-year old, be prepared for a citation and a thousand dollar fine! The checkpoint was an ingenious way to fatten the county's slush fund and payrolls. Why tax when you could use a mirror and a Fatty Ticket? And while doing so, turn the neighborhood folk into healthy, spindly, poor people.

Like a radar speed trap or the alcohol breath monitors, the wavy fun house mirror was moved from Coney Island to Fatty Island. The fat patrol siren would sound and your car was stopped. "Will you all step out of the car please," the fat inspector said, "This test is non-invasive, unlike the x-ray tests at the airport. This isn't even a pat-down test, no touchy, no feely. Please stand in front of the magic mirror. See yourself tall and thin as a string bean, or fat and squat as a roly-poly. Your weight doesn't matter, your mirror image does."

You could laughingly look at yourself in the mirror and become tall and thin and then fat and squat. The photographer on scene and the fat patrol cop would wait patiently to snap your picture as a short fat person appeared in the mirror. There was little protest at court to the thousand dollar fine because

the judge would say when confronted, "a picture is worth a thousand words."

The county treasury filled up quickly, the rich, sometimes greedy citizens learned after only a few stops at the Obesity Check Point that, with a fun-house mirror image, it didn't matter what you really weighed.

"Let's just take while the taking's good," da government said.

Car travel suddenly stopped, gas consumption increased dramatically, schools closed, home schooling rocketed, small corner grocery stores closed, and huge fuel guzzling helicopter fleets became the norm. There was none of this silly, "drop the kids off at school" or busing anymore. Your home literally became your castle, teacher's jobs were lost and the state budgets were suddenly balanced.

Maggie's weight program for all citizens definitely prevailed, after all just look in the fun house mirror. National Citizen's Awards were bestowed upon the families in the communities who had shown the greatest progress in lightening up and exhibiting the empty wallet syndrome; very few politicians excluded of course.

Remember, "Life is a cabaret my friend." So become thin and spindly my friend and the ghost of taxes will be gone.

This the mirror can prove!

Chapter 22

Small business, hog wash. Have you ever mucked out a pig sty? Good luck to the town that relishes a sty or cow pad methane farm. Da codes wouldn't allow it. Step up to carbon, burn coal and many cellulose. You can keep your feet warm, Alaskans know it. Helter Skelter, what can we do? Our culture needs to limit usages, but economically. A paradox could be a need for jobs, but not any untoward jobs in the neighborhood. We can't all be street sweepers or giant claw garbage truck drivers. We can't all be gas pumpers, meter readers, or even shoppers. Shopping is truly a specialty and a high end skill set. Without shopping you might starve!

So, what is this business of automatons and robots? Aren't we allowed to still vacuum and sweep the floors? Can't we let a few wild horses or cattle stray into town? Put the rodeo back into the cities, give the cowpokes some jobs, and the crowd some thrills! The sanitation department could pass out pooper scoops for parade type activities and porta-potties for our new tepee camps. The Native American land is our friend, so are small crafts people, and the not so small but clean manufacturing jobs. For just about every manufacturing job, we create four spin off jobs. We manufacture tourists by tempting them to be looky looks and see the sights, but we can't all become tourist guides. So one of the real issues facing us is that we need semi-clean manufacturing now. Clean, but not too clean is the issue. Hiring, wages and competitive possibilities in our towns can first mean, get and then use ideas used by the "brainiacs" and entrepreneurs to begin producing goods and jobs. Some might say build local, manufacture for global, but buy more and more here. That is why skilled shoppers are so important.

Are you a shop local yokel? I hope so. Swiftly tariff any unfair overseas subsidized labor, and while you're at it, clean up and simplify our codes as well. Perhaps we can then compete effectively and overseas folk, including Asians, will want to create jobs and expand manufacturing into our villages in the U.S.A.

Could with fair planning and speedy approvals, jobs be created in Prineville, Oregon?

Steve Jobs may have said, "Google and see."

Chapter 23

If you are walking in space, you seem to be weightless. Our jogging impact is even less than walking in an impact crater on the moon. If you want to live a long life, look at this.

Anton would faithfully hike two miles a day along the beach. Anton and his wife Noanie would spend at least two weeks in the summer hiking Mucho Peakos in the Andes. With a child-like wit and a steel trap mind, Anton would even drive a tractor on his family farm. He could invent and make sugar cubes out of mounds of unprocessed sugar for his coffee. He could sail ships, but not boats; an ark but not a dinghy; and swim and float in the ocean, but only because it was salty. On shore he was a land lover and at sea a floater. Could he be a surfer too? Anton could use a harpoon, catch a wave and feed on baloney. But Anton's main claim to fame was walking. So what?

Anton celebrated his 100th birthday last June. What a role model for us antiques! Skinny Anton, this mountain man, is doing as well at chomping on bison burgers and slurping huge chocolate sundaes, as he is at walking. A complaint or two by his dietician wife, Noanie does no good. Anton continues devouring his bison burgers, which after all was a staple of the really early Americans.

Anton, please do not bound up to obesity, be politically incorrect, eat and walk, but do not smoke, even cigars, if the dietician is present.

Just keep walking in our neighborhood!

Chapter 24

You've got to have heart, miles and miles of heart. No burgers, no mayo, ain't something to relish. Drab, drab, drab, you could associate with boring, boring, boring. Eat hearty me lads and lassies; embellish, embellish, embellish. Of course do this over and over and over again in your neighbor-hood and avoid Obesity Check Points. The off street paths and hiking trails will keep you far away from the Car and Bike Obesity Check Stops. Walking can create a spindly figure, when diet and exercise salons are not available. Please don't overdo even if you relish burgers and shakes or burgers and pies.

Walk in your neighborhood and what do you see? Like a magnifying glass from high in the sky, placed in a slow glider plane or a balloon, your eyes seem to pop out. You see that down below there are trees and gardens of many varieties. Homes, old and new, appear in many styles. You might even find a castle or two. Please don't forget the cars parked by the curbs in many shapes, colors, models and styles. You can sometimes detect foreigners in your neighborhood, whose cars or trucks have Montana or Montreal, Canada license plates. Rarely do you behold a Sonora or Baja California license plate. Why?

Be very aware, on a cold, cold night or day, beneath a freshly parked car or truck you might find a warm home for cats, never dogs.

Perhaps on your walk you will see very strange two-legged walking things that look familiar and frequently talk. These folk are leashed by the hand and led by our four-legged friends. Think of their great legal powers. We have leash laws, don't we? And plastic bags used as toilets which will soon be outlawed. Witness the serious business of people walking.

In our neighborhood, eight dogs carefully lead a lady down the street. At crosswalks one of these canines jumps up into her arms and leads her across the street. There is a reason for white stripes painted across streets at the corners.

In our neighborhood it is said that you can LEAD a dog's life.

Try it, with people walkers.

Chapter 25

Down at Tiffany's Brunch Bar Gilda asked, "So, you think you know your neighbors? There may be a cannibal heir nearby. Certainly this couldn't be possible in a civilized society or in your village. But think of the Donner Party traveling West more than 160-years ago. One little girl traveling with her doll in the Donner Party fortunately was safe from those very evil, hungry cannibals. Starvation and therefore desperate desires can change a party and a civilization overnight, but what about their heirs and their vittles."

Every Thursday Gilda ate lunch with the triplets Trudy, Tessie and Tanya. Jessica and Helena were regulars at the table too. If these ladies and their sometime guests seemed sweet. They were not. It was the pattern of ordering food that shocked and terrified Gilda's friends. The pattern first came to their awareness after at least a year of these luncheons at Megan's Vegan Restaurant. Why would Gilda always order an arm of lamb and then look depressed when the split pea soup arrived? Gilda always said that she was a vegan with carnivore teeth, but nonverbally her expression told otherwise.

One day the aroma from the next door hamburger stand did Gilda in. She screamed and raced to the door. As her fangs seemed to protrude, her rush to the hamburger stand was almost too MUnCH! With a plain burger grasped in her fist, no lettuce, catsup, or onions needed, Gilda's teeth locked on. She seemed to calm down somewhat, but her actions confirmed their recurring

doubts. What should the triplets say? What should Gilda do? The little group was so much fun, but should their luncheons end, just because they now knew that a cannibal lurked in their midst?

Emergency starvation plans needed to be considered. Immediately the Texas, Tex Stake and Rib House down the block became the recovery zone. Vegan diet food policies were thrown out the window and old cattle and vampire fixations helped Gilda erase her cannibal dreams. The triplets and their group adjusted to their new barbecue setting because deep in their hearts they knew that Gilda wasn't a cannibal.

But what if she was a vampire? Tune in later.

Chapter 26

Howard is a real hunk. His fire helmet, the great big red hook and ladder truck, all polished and gleaming, helped his image too. Howard had many medals of valor for single-handedly pulling people and bodies out of raging fires. This guy used huge hoses to very successfully douse many a fire. As a cigar smoking, real cussing guy, there couldn't be a more charming fire fighter.

That was the problem, he was too charming. There were always scandals to suppress, along with real fires. But why?

There she was, Badelia, in her Victorian mansion, with her sophisticated fire alarm system. What this petite trick desperately needed was a guy to help baste her turkey for Thanksgiving. What better way to find a handsome fire fighter than to burn a steak in an oily, very hot frying pan? Smoke soon rose from her stove, setting off the fire alarm with sirens, whistles and bells.

Dripping with jewels and dressed to the nines, Badelia climbed up high on the roof. With flames crackling around her, our dame shed tears shouting, "Howard, come save me!"

She was soon to be a goner.

The red fire truck careened around the corner at high speeds. Howard and his hook and ladder were coming to the rescue. Missing cars and George's Taco Truck by inches, the fire truck skidded to a halt, just moments before hell fire would consume the town's duchess.

"Badelia, be brave!" shouted Howard as he jumped into the bucket and soared into the sky like a high speed winch.

Hose in hand and with a hook resembling a cherry picker, our handsome hero snatched life from the jaws of death.

The screaming Mimi's, not her turkey, nor her rescuer, had made her catch!

The hell with the old Victorian house and the truly fried turkey, complete with stuffing. The neighbors would pull together and create a new habitat for Badelia… and Howard. After all of this, the planning department made arrangements for the couple to cohabit at their new tent camp. Howard, with his blunderbuss and Badelia with her skillet, both said, "I can do," as the judge pronounced them husband and wife.

Would you, in our very quiet neighborhood, inhabit a tent or tepee?

Chapter 27

Captain Primitivo arrived in our village early in the morning, just in time to downgrade our neighborhood museum. Accreditation, hog wash! Our museum's concrete whale just needed a fresh paint job.

Slick Willie, our town carpenter told Primitivo, "Slop on some outdoor blue whale paint. Be authentic with the eye and tooth paint too. Get the water based paint and slap it on before our city fathers and our planning committee can environmentally harpoon our project. Damn the torpedoes Primitivo. Get the paint on. See if you can do this faster than building a Chinese city."

Captain, I bet you didn't know that our village has a museum, the Whale Museum, which looks out over the ocean and a long gone castle. Other neighborhoods have museums too. There's the Surfer Museum, the Cement Boat as a museum, the Indian Skull Museum with its John Douglas Toilet, and the Indian Reed Canoe Museum.

Great curiosity revolves around the expression of going to the John, but only Primitivo knows that the crapper is the handle, chain, and flapper arrangement; a true valve issue. Please don't ignore or forget the now expired Marijuana Museum with its display of Navy hemp rope, ancient Egyptian growers, and our founding father George Washington's involvement too.

What you hear about for the most part, are the fancy city museums. Unlike the neighborhood's tiny museums packed with local content and history

and ignored by the press, city museums get the spotlight..

Hello there city and county councils, do we need to have Primitivos to begin occupying our neighborhood museums, just to draw attention?

Instead Primitivo, who wouldn't give up, occupied the lighthouse, which had been an empty museum. "Beam me up Scotty," became the catch-word for putting the spotlight on our communities and planet. We might add that we don't need intrusive noisy helicopters spraying unknown chemicals and shining their bright light beams. Let's just put Primitivo into action and let the blue suits back on the beat in our neighborhoods' streets armed with their flashlight beams.

Bring back the old spirit of getting to know you. NOW.

Chapter 28

Housing, infill with a lack of clutter and few high density thorough-fares through our neighborhoods all add to our security. Speed bumps, a few potholes, and cul-de-sacs help satisfy our needs. Timeless, aging and modern housing can substantially help add to the character of our neighborhoods. Old Victorian homes, a few old farm water towers, barns, chicken coops, a converted tiny general store, and even a carriage house can contribute to our panache. Of course squirrels, raccoons, skunks, mountain lions, red tail hawks, hummingbirds, rats, people and their pets help fill our yards and nests.

Trumpet calls at midnight, at least a third of a mile seaward from our home, awakened our neighbors. Not only crashing waves, but honking, roaring sea lions, sing to our ears. Seals and sea otters play in the waves as our surfer dudes and dudettes become bait for our lively, silent great white shark.

Does the Surf Museum have a surf board on display with a part of it chomped off by our shark? Perhaps a few great white shark teeth are needed too. The siren wails and the ambulance rushes off to a nearby hospital. We can only hope that the new victim still has all their arms and legs. Thank goodness, we don't have a giant octopus nearby too!

Just off shore in a very deep, long ocean trench, to this day Russian Nuclear Submarines with their nuclear war heads may lurk; a truly menacing great white shark. How secure is anyone in our neighborhood with these sharks lurking only a few miles away? But what's the upside? Of course, the finest survey maps of this trench that we still use today, were drawn by the ancestors of our early West coast explorers: the Russian explorers of Fort Ross, California, U.S.A.

It's World War Two and up the Pacific Coast a sea-scoured tunnel in an ocean cliff hides a two-man, enemy, military submarine. This is not the yellow submarine of a Beatles' vintage song, but an armed submarine with a torpedo, out to kill our neighborhood folk in their fishing boats.

Our Italian immigrants, who arrived as a fishing armada in the 1920s, were not totally closed down and moved inland in the 1940s. This was the West Coast and the skinny Italian Stud Valter was not on shore yet. But a Japanese submarine, a few balloon bombs, a light shelling of our coastline and a fear of invasion was created. The end of this tragic story was obvious: internment camps.

Let's not do it again, terrorists or not!

Chapter 29

Starvation caused by the after effects of a tsunami, tornado, earthquake, hurricane, or who knows what, could be a major pending calamity.

Calamity Jane couldn't have found a better neighborhood, village, town, country or state, to spew her natural wrath. Clyde was sure that every natural event was caused by sunspots. Calamity Jane believed that her sunscreen lotion did the trick. In a calamity our town closed down, the village neighborhood needed to redeploy. Big Box stores began to close down for good.

But why?

Little gas, roads cracked and were destroyed. All our thoroughfares are now nothing but trails. But have no fear Mika is here, or back not to the horse and buggy, but to the bike.

"Can a motocross bike become useful too?" asked a Hell's Angel.

Tune in to our proactive city and county councils, who not only saw the light, but had adopted the slogan, Drill Baby Drill, for water and did! With food supplies dwindling and farmers finding it almost impossible to travel to their markets except by lettuce cart, our council's had a great insight.

As felons flooded into our county jails from our state pens, these felons wanted jobs. Fortunately, Hilda, the landscape lady on the town council, saw the needle in the haystack and knew the forest from the trees. She had a distant

relative, a landscape architect turned probation officer who was changing felons into farmers near New Davis Creek, Oregon. A call was placed and he was available. A hundred felons were quickly found.

In the early morning hours the felons walked out of prison, armed with their shovels, hoes, seeds and fertilizer, (no bombs involved). They walked with their one time landscaper who was not carrying a piece. Eight hours a day, five days a week these folk were somewhat happy. The felons could pretty much forget their incarceration during these farming hours.

The outcome? Wow, plenty of fresh vegetables for Jane's calamity and for all the felons too!

Gardens were started at the Civic Center Plaza in San Francisco. The city of Detroit started some gardens too. Hot houses and tent camps weren't too far behind.

Hilda said, "We need to prepare for emergency food shortages and the cities have land. Let's get out Karl's tractor and frac the soil. We can grow our food and then walk our produce to farmer's markets and grocery stores. We must prepare for potential emergencies like starvation."

Don't be too glib, there is starvation in many parts of the world. Damn the thoroughfare, keep or create farms that grow produce near bike paths.

Chapter 30

What makes you think that a $100 "Benji" will be enough to buy a loaf of bread in the near future? Will your pension or mutual fund be there when you need them? What about building a strong society? Buffy had an answer, buy American made Chicago nails and the nail guns would function longer and better. Horrors, who would want quality and longevity, when you could buy planned obsolescence by purchasing flimsy out of country products? Who would want employment and job levels to increase, when homelessness, fore-closures, distraught families and their neighborhoods could abound with grief!

I guess it's tenting tonight at the not so old campground. The down-trodden homeless, the druggies, and the dirty are there. There are very few rain showers or showers to take. I guess the rain has gone away.

Grumbles from the town folk, "We've put up with these flea infested homeless long enough, or they're just anarchists stirring up trouble," was rare.

Let's step into the shoes of the economically deprived. Take the almost slam dunk issue of being wronged by economic plunderers who have accumulated vast wealth. Look no further than some venture capitalists, some hedge funds, some investment bankers, and their sometimes over the top, tony attorneys.

Where do you get with some of these deep pocket folk? A possible lawsuit with a justifiable issue might bring you the reward of victory and the unenviable result of empty pockets. The economic rewards may not meet the

economic costs and they know it!

Back on the reservation, the tent camp, you may feel disenfranchised with very little room for your protest about meaningful issues. There are very few inexpensive forums available for petitions today. At times the town merchants also feel threatened too. These merchant and government turfs could be occupied or trespassed upon during protests.

The issues of freedom of expression are being tested and with the help of radio, old fashioned newspapers and the Internet, many of these issues can be heard, to some extent. Our neighborhood, within a mile of our city's confrontation sites, sits peacefully by, unthreatened but concerned about police being hurt, protesters being hurt, property being damaged, and worried about whatever civilized behavior may mean at this time.

How do you lead, along with your issues of consequence, and commu-nicate with our government and our public? You can speak for barely two or three minutes before our city council. You can petition the Federal Courts, particularly on Constitutional Rights and freedom of assembly issues.
You can try to interact with da mayor, his teams and significant others.
Our town did this with little injury to folk, except perhaps to some free spirits.
Now the issues may go before the Federal Courts.

A resolution to these issues should not be:"Gee! The tent camps are gone, therefore there are no issues or standing in the court."

Out of sight, out of mind, need not prevail! Measured answers are needed.

Chapter 31

If you choose to sail the high seas of depression, foreclosure, job losses, homelessness, and a lot of corruption, our village cognoscenti need to understand leverage and derivatives, to the tune of more than fifty TRILLION dollars.

Go to your neighborhood bar, bank and casino in Chicago. Go to Heidi's Bar. Google the site and you might gain a simple, clearer picture of what derivatives really are.

So what? Many big banks in our cities play the not so un-risky game of, "Let's bet on almost thin air and hope that the counterparty on the bet isn't broke or let's bet on which way interest rates may go."

In a much smaller and closer-to-home way to help you understand derivatives, is to ask yourself the question, "Can I pay the home mortgage?" If you and many of your neighbors can't pay the mortgage, you have just become the almost broke counterparty.

Shift now to an expansive world that you may not know. Vast sums of money are constantly being borrowed by industry, government, pension funds, hedge funds, etc. Not all of these counterparties can just print money, although a few can, like the government and the F.E.D.! Oh, Wow! A loaf of bread could shortly cost one hundred dollars. It's called inflation!

So what happens in a world of havoc? It's happened before.

Prepare yourself for a barter economy. It's already happening here and there.

Burning Man at the Black Rock Desert is a one week, 50,000 people, test case of the bartering system. Can bartering be done on a large scale? World history thinks so! Traders in today's world have lost millions and/or billions of dollars at some banks, some hedge funds, some venture capital groups, and some investment banks, with their trading desk, if any. All hail to the computer driven algorithmic programs which do have a speedy advantage for sometimes stacking the deck. For most of us who just don't understand and can't remember the government's and your Solyndra Corporation's IOUs, for a solar company with an unpaid bill of more than a half billion dollars, there are definitions.

Back at Heidi's Bar in Chicago, she gets a credit call from her bank and her loan comes due. She makes some calls to her many customers with bar tabs outstanding. But the Harrys and Marys of the world drown their sorrows in suds and booze at Heidi's Bar. Their pockets were empty and they couldn't repay. Sound familiar? Heidi was broke too.

On and on, upward and onward to the banks and others.

Chapter 32

Investment bankers and others can make huge commissions when cities, counties and states create desperate needs.

Suffocating by pollution or becoming too thirsty for water and the threat of drought, are motivations for action. The seeds of fear are planted and it's a cake walk to desalination bonds, carbon credits, or clean coal and other alternatives. No one in their right mind likes pollution, or being thirsty in a drought, or being hungry in a famine. Few people enjoy higher special district taxes and taking taxes. The balancing point, not the tipping point, could include reasoned economic costs, including risks to your health and welfare.

The Chinese have just purchased close to 200 copies of a $90 book dealing with specialized hydrologic drilling into the aquifer, by Bill Bisson. Canada, Mexico and Trinidad are considering using, or are already using, these specialized drilling techniques. Satellite surveys are critical to a more economical means of water retrieval other than desalination. Santa Barbara sold at a deep discount, loss, its desalination plant to a mid-eastern country, where desalination is practical.

Can we have economic common sense? Probably not. The power is in the money and the commissions. As Jess Unruh said of power and politics, "Money is the Mother's milk of politics."

In certain areas, handicapping people with nonsensical rules on doing, is much like removing arms and legs from a runner just before a track meet. Hobble ingenuity and there is little, if any choice, but to pick up sticks or factories and leave, a state or country.

The Chinese listen to people in the Headwater Corporation because the Chinese have big, oppressive pollution problems. Dirty coal can be cleaned somewhat, but at a price, so the clean energy alternatives are appealing and may prevail over time. Concentration of sunlight focused onto mirrors, which then heats water to steam producing electric energy does have appeal. Algae conversion to fuel is another promising alternative energy.

We must be alert to the Federal Energy Regulatory Commission (FERC), attempting to decommission the clean, cheap, non polluting hydro-electric projects near Redding, and other northern California communities. Is this too a fishy project, as may be the removal of and termination of a long standing oyster farm, in order to save the pup seal? The pups are there now and have been for many years. Let's close down jobs employing human beings and create more unemployment!

Keeping an unbiased ear to the ground on downstream technologies that could prevail is difficult. Let's place some of our emphasis on the folk who actually measure pollution. "Midac," a small group located in the now defunct, buggy whip capital of Springfield, Massachusetts comes to mind. Can the eye in the sky Fastwood at the Net Propulsion Lab help too?

Maybe it's too late. I hope not.

Chapter 33

Hoboes and homeless are not synonymous, but can be interchangeable For the luminary, the homeless don't want to be homeless and may not want to be transients.

Harold, a semi-homeless guy, had his collection point next to a U.S. mailbox near a free parking lot. Folks would park their cars there and then walk to nearby shopping areas. Sixty percent of the folk would walk right by Harold sitting there on the sidewalk with a tree for a backrest. Most shoppers ignored Harold's needs despite having free parking. There were some who would drop a quarter or spare change into Harold's cupped hand.

Why is this important? Harold knows the homeless need help. Do you think for the most part that the homeless can get jobs? Think again.

Da new mayor, Day Train, might have had a brainstorm of an idea. Paint two parking meters orange, like the sunshine and let Harold be a meter tender also. If Harold is given the power to ticket cars when any meter expired, the city could pay Harold an extra twenty percent of the fine in their new tender, organic veggies. But let's not stop there. Harold would figuratively own the revenue from the orange meters. The coin collector for the city could count the meter change and immediately disperse organic veggies from the taco and veggie truck.

Harold now has two sources of income and a job! He's also present to observe purse snatchings and other malicious behavior. Better yet, Tammy and Timmy Dogooders, by parking at an orange meter could rejoice that they are helping create new jobs, feeding the homeless, and just feel good about partially halting starvation. Da Mayor could visualize one hundred orange parking meters, fifty new jobs and a lot of revenue enhancement. After all, Harold and his friends could get steady vegan income from the meters. Ticketing enhancements, up and down the blocks would become enormous sources of revenue for the city. Why? Harold and his friends were very, very alert and loved to ticket cars at expired meters.

A bummer for the parkers, but screw them for the common good!

Chapter 34

Branding a neighborhood could be a great idea. Or do we blend a neighborhood's individuality and personality into the bigger picture of a city?

East side, west side and all around the downtown, the city paid a bundle of money for a signage report done by outside professionals, who advised just that: East Side, West Side. Before doing this signage, we might ask, "Does the city even know where the borders of our East Side, West Side annexed neighborhoods are?" Why?

If you don't know what you've bought, how can you even begin to guide our neighborhood's future? Heavy thinkers care more for the bright lights of downtowns, shopping centers, and the traffic flows on roads with pot holes. Remember our neighborhood contributes property taxes to the county, good money for garbage disposal and a myriad of other taxes too.

Size of population groups, can be important too. Plato, the Greek believed that 6,000 people were enough to manage, even without cell phones and the Internet. Does a population of 60,000 folk become so cumbersome that guiding them becomes a real chore and their voices become hard to hear?

There are answers.

Town councils can meet with their television crews in distinct neighborhoods every month. With twelve neighborhoods, at least yearly visits to each one is possible. These forums, if well advertised in advance, could create

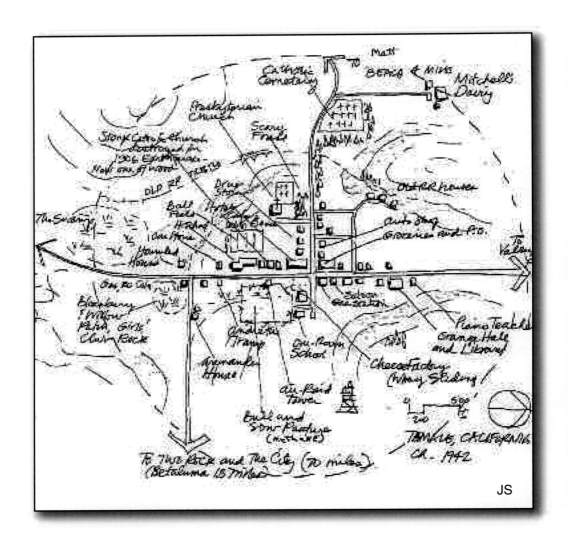

untold stories, ideas, and exciting energies for people where they live, a SoHo feeling, a Greenwich Village, a Harlem feeling, or a Spanish Harlem feeling, might emerge to vie with the Times Square syndrome. A public forum would allow more than a two minute period for folk to express their opinions. For example, the Beebright Neighborhood, with its ocean, lighthouse and whale museum, could be discussed.

Bring back the Bilkington tent camps of the 1880s in the area around the whale museum, or better yet at the Marine Lab. Reintroduce the railroad station, the castle, and occupy the vacant light house.

"Beam me up, Scotty!"

Chapter 35

Our not so neighborly neighbor Victor, had several prime objectives that guided his life: never own a home, never have a mortgage, never rent an apartment, never own a condo, or own a jet stream trailer, and never, ever live in a tent! Was this traumatic for his frequently bikini clad bride Tan-Fastic, even after 30-years of marriage? Their homelessness was not as harsh as you would expect.

This homeless dude grew up in the armpit or dust bowl of anywhere. With a promising, very low level job in a high tech company, Victor realized that he didn't speak their language. Night school, studying and a new degree in Electrical Engineering and Voila, Victor now speaks their language! He finally had a great salary scale, his beautiful bride Tan-Fastic, but still no house.

A call from a pal in New York City offering an interview for a potential job at five times what he was earning, created the need for a next day flight to the bright lights. Walking into the lobby of the manufacturing company Victor saw 24 applicants for the one job. Victor's uncle who headed the draft board in the job recruiter's neighborhood suddenly became quite helpful in Victor's job search.

After the first four applicants were rejected, it was Victor's turn to be interviewed. He walked into the recruiter's office and announced, "The 19 applicants still waiting in the lobby will not be interviewed for my new job.

Thank you so much for my new position with your company. I'll start tomorrow! Oh, by the way, if you should change your mind, or have any second thoughts, your forged application for military duty in Albania will be accepted! You will then leave for Albania, via Transylvania, immediately."

After a few years working for the Bra Manufacturing Company, Victor got edgy to move on. When a territory in northern California became available, Victor jumped at the chance to have an all expense paid move to the West Coast.

Shortly thereafter, the new fully licensed Captain, accompanied by Tan-Fastic, started their own ship and boat sales company at our neighborhood harbor. If you needed a canoe, rowboat, water ski boat, yacht, sailboat, new or used, you got them; the Captain made sure. But they cleverly managed to get more. The expensive luxury yacht owner, who was rarely onboard most of the year, begged Victor to be his security guard at the rate of $4,000 a month plus expenses.

This habitually homeless couple, Victor and Tan-Fastic, never regretted, nor turned down the opportunity to travel the high seas in style.

Sometimes homelessness is not as harsh as you might expect!

Chapter 36

Safety is a very important need at our neighborhood's grammar school, including the exposed crosswalks at its signal lighted intersection. Here our hidden 79-year old hero, Wayne, is the traffic monitor.

For twenty-one years Wayne has been vital in keeping school children safe from the dangers of careless bikers and cars passing through the busy intersection. Just having signal lights didn't cut it! Rolling cars stops and the yellow light intersection runners made Wayne's job a must. Add people talking or texting on their cell phones and his job was mandatory.

The city's proactive town council and police department was completely perceptive in hiring Wayne. Winter, summer, spring, or fall, Wayne, not a couch potato, answered the call. Saving a child from harms' way, at least once a month, put him in danger, but he always put duty and safety first. Wayne, in sunshine or storm, was a traffic monitor. With one hand holding his stop sign, his other hand available for a young child, and with a severe glare for the errant driver, he did his work.

Wayne's beat is the crosswalk, signal light control and children walking to and from school. Can you envision a volunteer with a whistle, who would not only save a child, but be there for children every school day come rain or shine, for twenty-one years! What a hero's hero. Even the mayor realized that Wayne was not a 911, fire fighting hero type, but was an unsung, unacknowledged hero none-the-less.

Wayne may someday receive the Mayor's medal of great service, a free pass to the movies for a year, and a not so silent appreciation from the parents and teachers of the Gully Grammar School. Wayne's life says everything. We thank you Wayne, our hero, for saving and protecting our children's lives. You truly reflect what our neighborhood and your heart is all about, LOVE!

Chapter 37

Today's the day to pass the time away, writing difficult thoughts into your mind. What clutter we can have, like stacks of books at home or the need to fill the mind with Googles. But is it true that if you're ignorant, you're trying too hard?

Ignorance is great because everyone can use it freely. The more ignorance you learn, the more your ignorance can expand. That's the only way your ignorance expands.

It's like the expanding universe and the expanding mind. Some people don't try to expand their ignorance, they keep a little ball of it.

A motto might be, if you don't know anything, you don't realize it. You might say, "It's a waste of time being an amateur epistemologist. But you are aren't you?"

Hoolu, the guru, smashed a knitting machine because he loved Lilly Putins, paddle wheels, and his wife. To Tarsha, the tree hugger, knitting was her life. And as the sledge hammer brought the knitting industry to a thudding halt, except in parts of Asia, Tarsha's life in the Vladivostok of the USA, substantially improved.

Colorful, hand-knitted hats to warm the brain, fired our minds with spark-like dreams of yesteryear. This indulgent beauty believed that she was in a rainbow- like yarn. Perhaps in an old sailor's yarn that could go on and on.

Tarsha weaved her spells and hats, which brought back, buy locally humanness and clarity to our neighborhood. The heat of the hats got the wind-mills of our minds turning our town upside down. Suddenly, ten neighbor-hoods reemerged as if out of nowhere and sparked the excitement that ignorance can bring. After all, nobody knew where our neighborhoods exactly are; where we live! Go ask the town fathers and mothers if they do. Ask Hoolu and Vlad the Impaler who the Lilliputians and the LUDDITES are.

Windmills of the mind

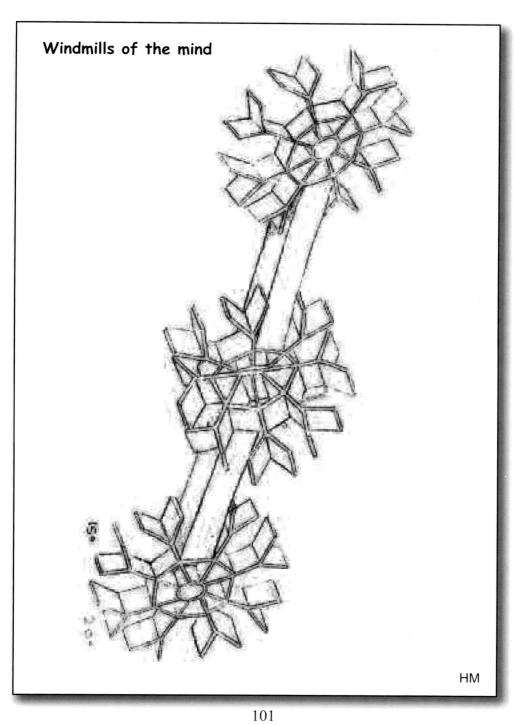

HM

Chapter 38

They say the wind's Mariah. The chief blew into town after a 26-mile run. The grizzled, weathered, 75-year old runner sat down on the bench in front of a trapper's 1880s brick building, now a famous bookstore and vegan coffee shop. Prepared for any hippies and high taxes-tax collector, Hiawatha's cigar store, not so wooden Indian, Black Cloud began a rain dance where he hoped to get a little fire water from the sky or elsewhere.

As I sloshed through the mud to the dry ground of the bench in front of the old brick building in order to talk with him, Black Cloud prepped his bow and arrow to shoot any straggling Burners or Coyotes from out on the playa. Many a hunter's pickup truck mysteriously ended up with an arrow or two in its side panel. You see Black Cloud was nearsighted and he thought he saw deer grazing by. The sheriff set up road blocks for the hunter, but never discovered the source. Even the highway patrol came up empty handed.

Down and dirty, after three hours of conversing with Black Cloud, the Paiute's lore and wisdom bloomed, almost as if a Wizard was there. As the story sadly goes, almost no one on the reservation excelled beyond high school.

Black Cloud said, "White Wing flew through a very high end, advanced physics degree at the University of Florida, and then with a law degree, set her shingle out in Missouri."

Folk in the area questioned Black Cloud's credibility, but some of us knew that he was a true straight arrow. After all he never missed a truck panel. We also know that a father's story about his daughter has got to be true.

All this conversation, followed with the conundrum of what to do or not to do, in the presence of a great Indian Chief. Of course! Straighten up and fly right, "Smile Black Cloud, so I can take the great and mandatory picture of you."

Black Cloud replied, "That'll be five bucks, not braves, for the picture and another five for the smile." A frozen face is expensive and fire water is too.

The rain came down and sadly the fire water did too. So much so that hitching a ride in any pickup truck became impossible. The 26-miles back to home grew longer and longer in his mind and a few warm haystacks seemed almost as comfortable as his tepee.

Black Cloud has now passed into the big sky and I can only wonder if he will find the waters in the sky as warm as the memories of his frozen face.

Chapter 39

What a horrible week in our cul-de-sac. My wife, Sabrina, lost her parrot to the sky. She has gone into deep mourning, black window drapes and all. Two weeks later she was still at it, bawling huge teardrops and fasting! One was at their wits' end as to what to do. Was it the ambulance, fire truck or morning paper?

That morning the fog was heavy, the newspapers were too, and down the street in the foggy mist appeared the beautiful Cherise, in her negligee. She was attempting to herd, with no luck, Benji, a strutting rooster, to safety behind a neighbor's white picket fence.

The neighborhood came to the rescue, or maybe it was just me, to help the damsel in distress. After fifteen minutes of eyeing, and herding Benji, with his beautiful green, black, orange, yellow, and red colored feathers, I decided there must be other, more productive things to do.

With a fleeting farewell glance at Cherise, back I went to the high fenced yard and the black window shades of the gloom and doom hovel, where Sabrina was bawling. It took far more than the Gift of God to budge Sabrina, before the mourning light dawned on me!

"Sabrina, I do have a surprise for you out in the street. Come on, hurry up, come see!" I called. With hard, pleading and coaxing, Sabrina walked in her PJs, out into the street and gasped, "Oh!"

Benji, made a B-line rush toward Sabrina. Sabrina rushed to scoop up Benji, suddenly as if the rooster was hers all along. Giving the rooster a big hug, Sabrina stopped crying.

Benji could do no wrong. He was truly the cock of the walk. The back of the living room couch, the living and dining room tables were all fair game for this wannabe raptor. Even our dogs knew Benji ruled the roost. They kept their distance! Benji had his own chicken coop in the small, high fenced, front yard where he resided on many a day. Sabrina made sure that the chicken coop was very luxurious, with many amenities and feeding troughs. Clean hay was spread every day.

A real shocker occurred near the end of the month when twelve eggs appeared in the coop.

Sabrina, in shock, immediately painted the coop pink.

Goodbye Benji. Hello BONITA!

Chapter 40

Now the day is over, night is drawing near, shadows of the evening steal us off to dream. When our eyelids begin to droop, our neighborhood can still maintain. Shut off the forced feeding, smart meters, close off the cell phones and prepare for the tougher duty of dreamland after the late night show.

Dream of a neighborhood with borders clearly outlined, even if you live on the east side or west side, or the north side or the south side of Chicago, or anywhere around our towns. Why be a zombie in a trance getting lost?

Your city already is!

For property taxes and refuse, they've got you pegged, but ask about a neighborhood and its borders and it becomes inane. No records! Ignore a neighborhood, which occupies a space, being a somewhat pleasant spine of our cities, and the peril of indifference raises its ugly head. Could the neighborhood be in the east or the far west?

Da mayor, Day Train, cares about his city too, because he knows approximately where the neighborhoods are. The hell with it, if the city doesn't know where our neighborhoods are, we'll just pretend to know. After all, we do know where we live!

Isn't it fun to explore and embellish our lives and where we really live? Whether you spend your time in an arrondissement, borough, village, or even an old time bar, you can barter if you need to, if and when your credit and credit cards go away. Bank on a new form of trade where some bankers tend to their pens, and leave some traitors or some traders for another sentence or two. But after "too big to fail" is gone, guess what, we're almost all still here!

Goodnight Dreamers, continue to build a vibrant life. Beam me up or down, or north or south, east or west.

Beam me up, Scotty!

OCEAN

BAY

SCHOOL

CHURCH

BAR

TO NEXT
SMALL TOWN

TO

GAS STATION   CITY

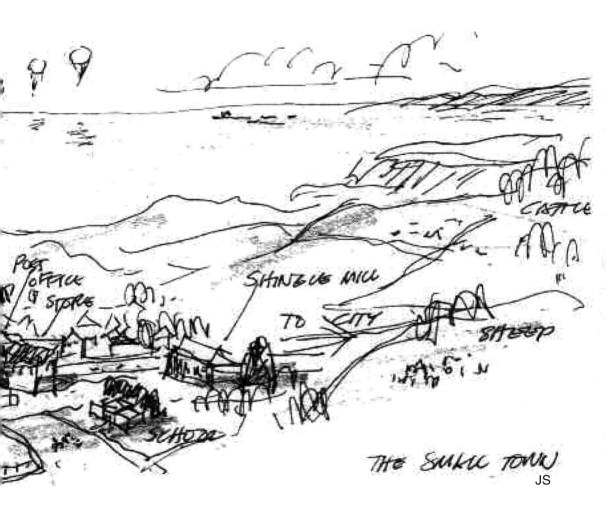

POST OFFICE & STORE

SHINGLE MILL

CASTLE

TO CITY

SHEEP

MAGNIN

SCHOOL

THE SMALL TOWN

JS

113

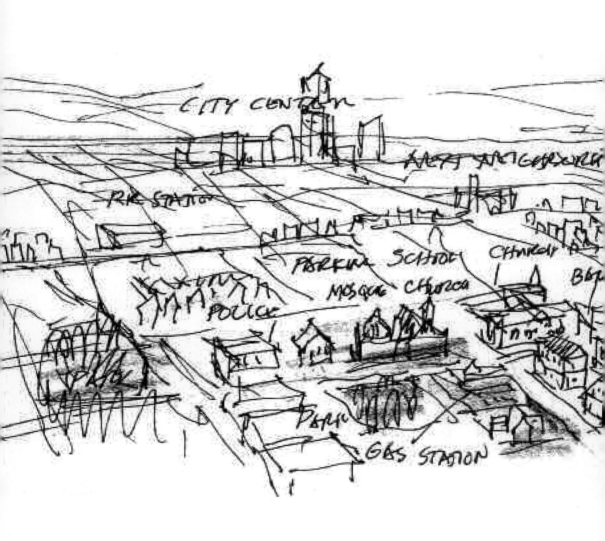

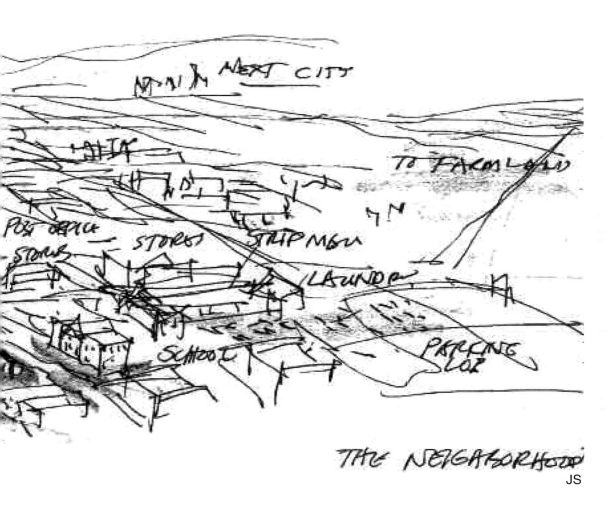

THE NEIGHBORHOOD

JS

Acknowledgements -- really thank you!

Illustrators:
Jack Sidener, FAIA
Jessica Brook Curnow-Rahm, HM

Editor: Jean Bilodeaux
Photographer: Jeff Morse, LH
Painter: Drew Lewis, Renaissance Man
Consultants: Marsha and Hugh Gregg

For information or copies contact:
Penn Schaw
P.O. Box 164
Homewood, CA 96141

ISBN 978-0-9851512-0-1

Printed in Hong Kong